Advance Praise from Amazon readers for *Garry's Upside-Down Adventure!*:

Look no further for a fun, wickedly smart children's book. Garry's Upside-Down Adventure is sure to grab the attention of even those young ones who are most determined to not enjoy reading a book.
—AMANDA ADAMS

This is the perfect book to help family's bond together. I really loved gargoyles as a kid, so when I saw this book, I couldn't help but feel it would be a great story to share with my daughter. The two of us had fun reading through it at bedtime.
—CHELSEY MCQUITY

The Adventures of Garry The Gargoyle's, graphics are so well done and the story is so cute. Parents will enjoy reading this to their kids. It will definitely spark a child's imagination.
—K. PUCK

Garry's Upside-Down Adventure is an incredibly sweet and cute book that both my kids and I enjoyed! The illustrations are done very well with great quality and attention to detail, and they help bring the written story to life. It was funny, educational, and had a good storyline with a sweet ending. I will definitely keep my eye for more in this series and other books from this author!
—CORRIE M.

It caught my attention when I saw the illustration on the cover but I did not imagine the wonderful universe that it kept inside. The dedication and effort put into each illustration is evident and makes the book a beautiful journey, in addition, the story is beautifully written, in a language that even is aimed for children, an adult enjoys it greatly too. A beautiful story with a gargoyle as a protagonist that entertains both adults and children.
—ANAMARÍA AGUIRRE CHOURI

I was captivated by this story of Garry... I think this is the ideal story for parents to read with their children or for a teacher to share with a class of grade school students. The Author, does a fantastic job of telling the tale of Garry's adventures. She brings him to life with her creative vocabulary and was thoughtful enough to include a Glossary of the words that have historical meanings. I would recommend this book for young children or young at heart adults. I am confident all will enjoy Garry's adventures.
—KRYSTALLYNE

Garry's Upside-Down Adventure!

ILLUSTRATED BY
PAISLEY HANSEN

WRITTEN BY
KARIN VARDAMAN

THE ADVENTURES OF GARRY THE GARGOYLE ~ BOOK 1

Garry's Upside-Down Adventure
The Adventures of Garry the Gargoyle—Book 1

ISBN: 978-1-948638-68-5

Page design by
Fideli Publishing, Inc.
119 W Morgan St
Martinsville, IN 46151

www.FideliPublishing.com

Published by

Shamlaigh Media
Denver, CO

PRINTED IN THE UNITED STATES OF AMERICA

Dedication

To Mom,

May the winds of heaven blow between the ears of your horse...

I love you.

Mary Christenson Wyman

A Wee Bit of Info...

Garry: Derived from the medieval name Garrett, meaning hard or bold spear.

Historical character traits for the name 'Garrett' include: bold, sturdy, solid, curious, imaginative, adaptable, introspective, averse to restriction, and possessing a strong sense of duty. Those with the name 'Garrett' may be nervous and seek peace and harmony. They need the love of family and friends.

Gargoyle: Middle English term derived from the Old French word gargouille, which means 'throat.'

The name 'Gargoyle' evolved from the French legend, La Gargouille, the origin story of gargoyles. A version of this mythical tale is shared within this book.

Shamlaigh: Shamlaigh (Sham-lay) is a variation of the Irish Gaelic word, Samhlaigh, meaning imagination, and is the fictitious town featured in this story.

This name was chosen not only because of its befitting meaning, but also in honor of the creator of *Garry The Gargoyle*—my mom, who appreciated her strong Irish heritage, and held a deep love of the culture.

The Adventure Begins

Shamlaigh, 1955

The Gothic cathedral towered over the township of Shamlaigh—a reminder of times long ago. To those passing by, it was just an old church in the middle of a modern city. But to Garry, the ancient cathedral was home—home for nearly five hundred and two years.

Who is Garry, you ask? Why … Garry is one of many gargoyles who lived UP, high along the stone walls of the historic church. And, like all gargoyles, he had the most important job of diverting rainwater away from the granite building through his cleverly crafted mouth.

If you've ever spoken with a gargoyle, you know they delight in showing off their ability to spout water, often holding contests to see which gargoyle can squirt water the farthest. And, though Garry was rather squat for a traditionally carved stone creature, he could keep up with the best of them, spurting rainwater far and away from the tower upon which he perched. Garry remembered a time when humans far below stopped during the heavy rains and gazed up in awe at the many flowing gargoyle fountains high above. Sadly, these days, no one below seemed to care anymore—too busy with their lives as they rushed here and there. But the gargoyles remained loyal to their duties, protecting the cathedral masonry through each passing century.

Besides performing as waterspouts, gargoyles held a second job—a job Garry didn't much like. You see, most gargoyles are carved with ugly faces to scare away evil spirits threatening the building upon which they crouch—but Garry had no desire to be fierce. Though he could feign a ferocious face scary enough to spook even the most wicked of evils, Garry was much more interested in making friends than frightening things away. The truth is, Garry preferred to spend time squawking with the ravens gliding over the spire, or warbling with songbirds roosting on the tower ledge next to him. He particularly looked forward to watching the pulsating waves of butterflies as they fluttered by each spring in shimmering clouds of turquoise, magenta, and gold.

During the warm summer nights, Garry often made himself dizzy trying to talk with moths that swirled around his head seeking the light of the moon. And he so enjoyed the spiders' company as they spun their elaborate webs, hoping to catch a meal before sunrise. But, even with the birds, butterflies, spiders, and other gargoyles to keep him entertained, Garry grew bored. *Five hundred and two years is a long time to be stuck in one place, atop an old church.*

Thus, the story of Garry's first big adventure begins—his UPside-DOWN adventure!

Centuries ago, when Garry first came to be, heroic knights rode on grand horses and beautiful princesses strolled the cobbled square adorned in flowing, silk gowns, with glittering jewels braided in their hair. Flickering lanterns lit up the town at night, and lively music could be heard from the taverns in the square.

But, that was then.

Garry understood the world as it was when he was first carved. But throughout the many ages, everything in the world had changed. Now, all appeared strange—and, none of it made much sense to him. For hundreds of years, he watched from his lofty station as the horses, fancy ladies, and fire torches that once glowed along dusty streets slowly disappeared, all replaced by speedy, horseless carriages, peculiar buildings, and strange noises. Garry was bewildered and fascinated at the same time—nothing was the same, except for him and the old church he called home.

One day as Garry contemplated the world below, he had an idea—a marvelous idea! "I'm tired of being UP when the rest of the world is DOWN! I want to take a closer look at all of those little people, little houses, and little trees! Oh, there is much I could explore in the world of DOWN!"

So, Garry decided to go.

One night, after the moon rose round and bright, Garry the Gargoyle detached himself from his centuries-old home and, using his clawed hands and clawed feet, braved the long climb to DOWN. As he passed by the other gargoyles, they warned him not to go, teasing him, calling out to him, and telling him he'd be sorry. "Don't be daft, Garry," one gargoyle bawled. "A gargoyle's job is to sit on the cathedral and squirt rainwater!"

"It has always been that way, and no gargoyle should try to change it," a second gargoyle piped up.

"Nothing good can come of this," a third gargoyle warned.

But, Garry was determined, and down, DOWN, DOWN he went!

What can possibly go wrong? he deliberated. *All of those humans, houses, and carriages that go by without horses are so tiny—they couldn't possibly hurt a small gargoyle like me.*

At last, the climb to DOWN was over. Garry dropped onto the landing in front of the grand doors of the cathedral just as dawn broke in dazzling sparkles of amethyst, coral, and fuchsia. Eager to finally examine DOWN up close, Garry surveyed the view, but...

Nothing was as he imagined it would be!

You see, from Garry's view from atop the cathedral, everything DOWN appeared so very small. But, now, the people weren't little, the houses weren't little, and the trees weren't little. Garry had to look UP to see everything! Well, almost everything—only a thin church mouse that scuttled across Garry's foot was smaller than he was. For all of his life, Garry had looked DOWN—down at the buildings, down at the carriages, and down at the people.

And now...EVERYTHING was UP!

Down Instead of Up!

Garry shuddered from the tips of his pointed ears to the bottom of his calcite feet as he looked around him. Shamlaigh was so busy and loud with countless people racing to and fro. Horseless carriages zoomed by, frightening Garry as he wrinkled his nose at the stench of ashen smoke puffing from the roaring vehicles.

What have I done?

Garry returned his attention UP—up to the top of the church tower and the sun-bleached steeple where he had lived and felt safe for hundreds of years. Maybe the other gargoyles were right, he thought. Maybe it was a mistake to leave my post. *This DOWN instead of UP thing is terrifying! Perhaps, I better go back UP before something bad happens. But, UP is quite far away, and the journey to DOWN was no doddle.*

Weary, Garry leaned against the church wall, closing his eyes to better think. True—he was afraid. But, he was also something else...

8

Curious.

He finally had the chance to explore DOWN—so, in spite of being really, REALLY scared, Garry put his fears aside and decided to stay.

Excitement swelled within him as he hopped down the five steps to the sidewalk below. *That was jolly good fun!* Except, upon landing, Garry had plopped right in front of the elderly Mrs. Darcy, an elegant but frail lady wearing a frilly hat and a ring on every finger. And... her giant, butterscotch-colored Great Dane!

Intrigued, Garry smiled his most jovial gargoyle grin at Mrs. Darcy, showing off his impressive fangs—and, he even smiled at the dog. But, yikes! Mrs. Darcy shrieked and the Great Dane growled, his sharp teeth snapping at Garry's head!

Garry froze (he was good at standing still, as all statues are), thinking the old lady and Mr. Butterscotch would realize he was just a harmless stone statue, and walk away.

But, that didn't happen.

Mrs. Darcy wailed as she gawked at the gargoyle while the Great Dane's canines nipped even closer to Garry's head. Reeling back, Garry's hands flailed in defense as more people gathered to investigate the cause of the uproar. Not knowing what else to do, Garry curled his lips to smile at them as well.

They cried out too!

I don't understand what all the fuss is about—I'm being quite polite! Baffled by the scene playing out around him, Garry's instincts warned him not to stay where he was.

So, he bolted.

Sprinting to nowhere in particular and as fast as his little gargoyle legs could carry him, he attempted to cross the street—but, one of the thunderous carriages screeched around him, its horn honking in protest. Garry skidded to a stop and cowered, holding his stony hands over his quivering ears. Then, a bald man in a blue uniform and a natty cap, standing in the middle of the street, pointing this way and that, tried to smack Garry with a wooden club.

Panic and confusion overwhelmed Garry and, to make everything worse, he realized he was lost in the city of Shamlaigh. Desperate to find a place to hide from all the terror of DOWN, Garry scanned the frenzied streets.

Then, he saw it...

On the opposite corner, he glimpsed a store appearing to contain all kinds of familiar things—items he had viewed while peeking through the scratched and cloudy attic windows of the cathedral--chairs with faded upholstery, oil and canvas paintings, and ornately framed mirrors dulled with time. Everything was old, just like Garry. *It's a sanctuary!* Except to reach it, Garry had to cross yet another street, avoiding the roaring carriages, humans trying to smack him, and dogs snapping at him—or any one of the other dreadful affairs of being DOWN. But the store seemed his only option, so the gargoyle ran as fast as he could, his six toes digging into the asphalt as he dashed across the harrowing intersection.

Upon reaching the shop, Garry launched himself right through its big picture window. CRASH, and landed with a loud THWACK on the wooden floor. You see, in his panic, Garry hadn't noticed the glass window. To him, it was an invisible wall.

He lay dazed, unsure of what had happened. Then, he rolled his eyes to the left and saw his ear, scattered in pieces all around him. *Oh, my!* Then, he rolled his head to the right and saw his right arm resting a foot away from his body. Garry winced. *Double oh, my!*

How did I let this happen? Why did I come DOWN from the safe UP of my steeple? I had a perfectly cantie gargoyle life.

And, now, he lay broken, alone, and lost.

Garry certainly felt as if his world had turned UPside-DOWN.

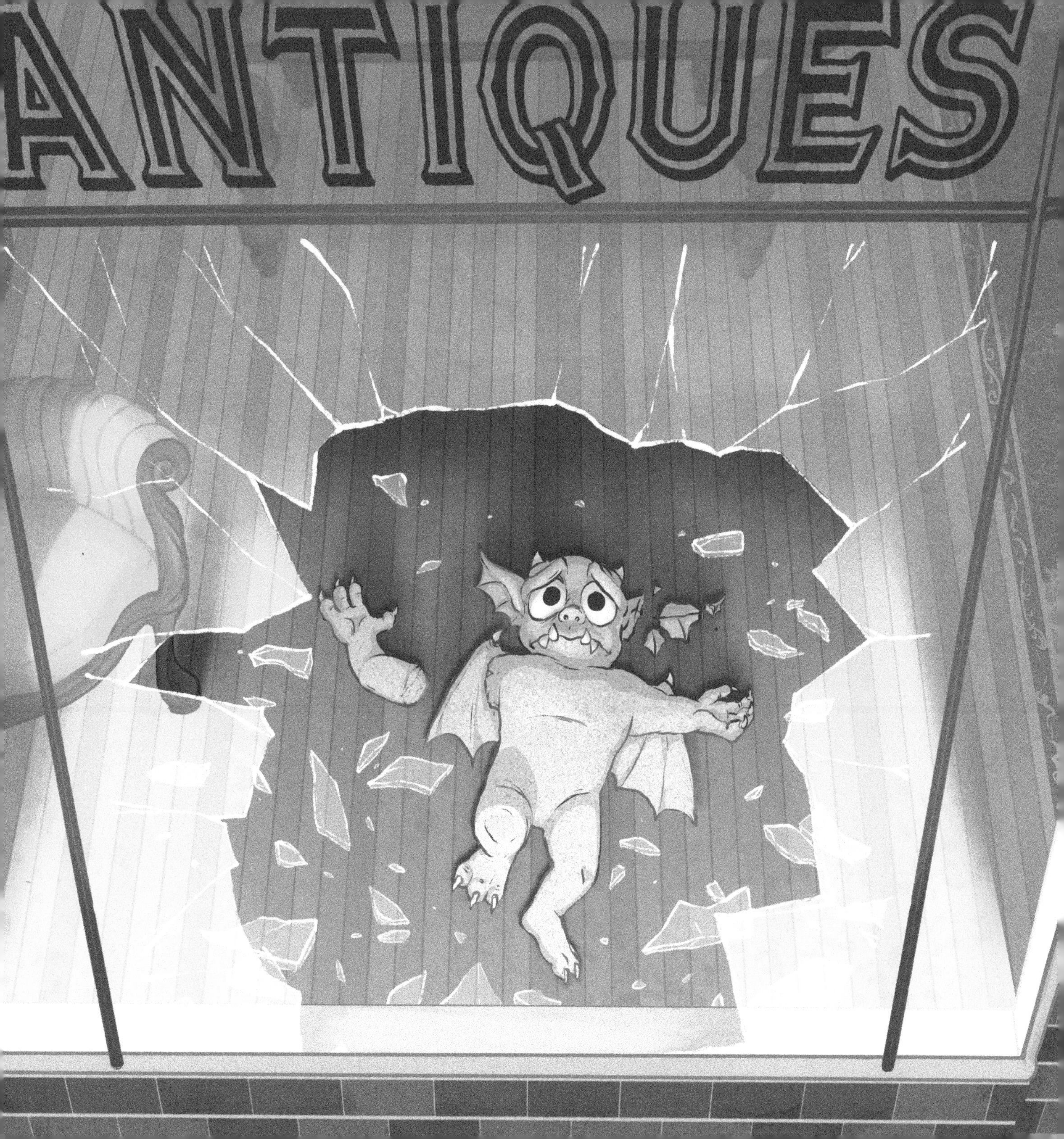
ANTIQUES

The Antique Shoppe!

"Good heavens! What happened here?" Mrs. Payne stood, stunned at the mayhem before her. The shoppe owner, who had sapphire eyes, impeccably-coiffed platinum hair, and a flare for fashion, entered her store to discover a little broken gargoyle lying on the wooden floor, surrounded by glass from the shattered window.

"Did someone throw this statue through the window?" Mrs. Payne wondered aloud as she stared at Garry. "But, why?"

Mrs. Payne lifted the gargoyle to its feet, examining it with an expert eye. "This gargoyle looks to be an authentic relic from the 1400s," she noted to herself. "Too bad it's damaged—otherwise it might have brought a good price in my shoppe."

Mrs. Payne collected Garry's broken arm as well as the pieces of his splintered ear, carrying it all to her workbench in the back of the store. There, she gently arranged Garry and his parts on a soft, periwinkle cloth. Lying there, he could hear Mrs. Payne fretting while sweeping up the broken glass, ashamed he had made such a mess. But Garry felt sorrier for himself, and what might happen to him now.

He lay awake on the comfy cloth throughout the night. In the morning, Mrs. Payne returned with a bottle of foul-smelling liquid. He didn't dare move. Drop by stinky drop, she used that smelly goo to glue all of Garry's broken parts back together. *She fixed me! I'm gobsmacked!* Garry suppressed the urge to whoop with glee.

Mrs. Payne then set Garry on the floor, inspecting his repairs. Satisfied, the owner of the antique shoppe positioned him in a prominent place right at the front of the store among various other things, some more antiquated than others. She then tied a tag around his neck upon which she wrote:

Antique gargoyle!
Price reduced due to damage!!!

Of course, Garry didn't know what that meant, or why he had been put in that specific spot—but at least he felt safe among the other old things, and grateful to be in one piece.

Several days passed as humans strolled in and out of the antique shoppe. Some browsed with interest, while others took only a quick peek on their way to elsewhere. A few customers even eyed Garry as he remained motionless in his assigned spot.

Then one morning, just as the shoppe opened for business, a black cat with luminous jade eyes cruised through the door, parking himself next to Garry. Startled by the unexpected visitor, Garry wanted to say hello but didn't know if cats could scream. The cat strutted around Garry, his eyes glittering in the sunlight. You'll do fine, the cat thought, and sidled up to Garry, rubbing against him while making an odd prrrring sound.

How rude! Garry didn't like that, at all. The cat sauntered back and forth against him, swishing his tail right under Garry's nose.

"Excuse me, cat—will you please stop that," Garry asked, keeping his voice low.

"Ohhhh, noooo..." the cat purred. "Your rough chin and stony legs are perfect for my massage.

"Please," Garry pleaded, "you're making my nose tickle. If I sneeze, it might scare the humans."

"I don't care..." The cat rubbed on Garry back and forth, back and forth. "Gargoyle, you are now my rubbing post, and you should feel honored I chose you."

"Why is that?" Garry's nose twitched.

"Because I am the cat—that's why. Prrrr..."

Garry could no longer contain the itch in his nose. KACHOO!!! The sneeze detonated with such force, the black cat jumped straight up into the air with a hiss! After landing with a thud on the table next to Garry, the cat scampered away, knocking off two bronze candlesticks that clat-

tered to the floor. The incident raised such a ruckus, Mrs. Payne rushed to the table to see what had happened.

Oh, no! Garry tried hard not to tremble. But when Mrs. Payne saw the cat scurry from the scene, she scolded it out the front door with a broom, not even giving Garry a glance.

To her, Garry was simply a gargoyle made of stone.

"That'll teach that moggy cat," Garry snickered.

Days passed.

Garry often daydreamed of his early years on the church steeple. *How magical the world seemed then, and how peculiar it was now...* And as he reminisced, noting the assorted artifacts chaperoning him in the antique store, a sense of melancholy washed over him. *Is this all I am? A meaningless token from the past in a modern world?* Garry slumped, his ears flopping like limp rags, despair overtaking him.

The Bug People

Each day, Garry tried to lift his spirits by watching customers wandering in and out of the antique shoppe. He mused about who they were, where they were from, and spun tall tales to himself about their lives. Then, one foggy afternoon, a man and a lady who were so tall they towered over the other customers entered the shoppe, capturing Garry's attention.

The gentleman wore round, black-rimmed eyeglasses with thick lenses that made his charcoal eyes look as large as teacup saucers. An olive cloak covered his lanky frame. He moseyed through the store, cocking his head with deliberation as he considered the many items for sale. Then, an image formed in Garry's mind. *By golly, he's a giant praying mantis bug man! How splendid!*

The man's wife, with her thin body and knobby knees, also provided fun for Garry. *She's a walking-stick insect lady,* he chuckled to himself, as the walking stick sashayed through the shoppe, looking as delicate as the keepsakes in the glass cases.

Garry continued to watch the bug people as they wandered about until, a few moments later, the praying mantis noticed Garry and paused.

Oh, no! I hope bug people don't eat gargoyles. Garry chuckled again.

The bug man approached Garry, peering at him with his magnified eyes. He then knelt in front of Garry, analyzing his every nook and cranny. Well, Garry no longer found humor in the bug man, and considered showing off his most sinister gargoyle face to scare the human away. However, since he didn't know how the bug man might react, he decided against the idea.

Suddenly, the bug man hoisted Garry off the table and set him on the counter next to Mrs. Payne. Help me! Garry wanted to shout out loud.

After a brief exchange of words, the praying mantis handed the shoppe owner some silver coins. Mrs. Payne then wrapped Garry like a cocoon in russet paper, and the praying mantis, with the walking stick at his side, carried Garry out of the antique store.

Garry's stomach flip-flopped at the sudden motion. *They ARE going to eat me! Oh, these dreaded collywobbles. Where am I going? What is happening to me?*

Then with horror, Garry realized he was being deposited into one of the ghastly cars. *I've been swallowed whole by a traveling beast!* Garry's anguish deepened as his mind sunk into reflections of home...

The home he believed he would never see again.

Garry gradually awakened from his trauma-induced stupor to find he was released from the paper-wrap. He had been set on the hearth next to a whitewashed brick fireplace. On a teak mantel above him sat a crystal vase overflowing with pink roses. The soothing scent of the flowers helped to ease Garry's tattered nerves as he cleared his head to consider his new situation.

The oblong room in which Garry found himself contained an assortment of human—not bug—furniture. An overstuffed, leather sofa occupied one wall, and a desk piled high with papers and books stood in the middle of the room. Watercolor paintings covered the otherwise drab beige walls.

As Garry studied all surrounding him, his curiosity crept back in. *Am I the first gargoyle to ever have been in a human house?* Garry considered. *This could be quite fascinating. Perhaps...I will like this part of being DOWN instead of UP!*

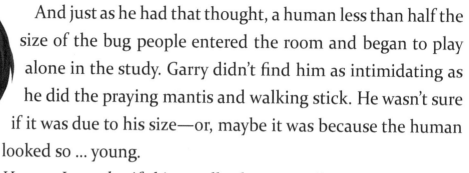

And just as he had that thought, a human less than half the size of the bug people entered the room and began to play alone in the study. Garry didn't find him as intimidating as he did the praying mantis and walking stick. He wasn't sure if it was due to his size—or, maybe it was because the human looked so ... young.

Hmm... I wonder if this smaller human will scream if I talk to him. Garry watched as the boy continued to stack his colored blocks. *Maybe he'll help me get back home. He looks tame enough.* So, Garry decided to risk gaining the boy's attention. "Hello..."

The boy's head whipped around, mystified by the unfamiliar voice.

"Over here!"

"You talk!" The boy screeched, staring at Garry in in disbelief.

"Please, don't yell," Garry begged.

The boy stood and marched over to Garry, his mocha, puppy-dog eyes filled with wonder. "My name is Thaddeus Stevens."

"My name is Garry."

No screaming. No shrieking. No growling.

After a moment or two of exchanging pleasantries, Garry explained to Thaddeus how he journeyed to Shamlaigh from the cathedral, including the events that brought him to Thaddeus's home. *Well, that was a jolly, good old chinwag. But, now it's time to get down to business.*

"Thaddeus, will you help me get back to my home?"

"Sure, I'll help you!"

Garry flaunted his jagged gargoyle teeth and Thaddeus laughed in return. Garry's heart lightened at finding a new friend in this Upside-DOWN world, and he knew now that everything would be okay.

"I'll help you, Garry..." Thaddeus cocked his head, thinking. "But, first, will you come meet some of my friends? They won't believe me if I just tell them about you. Please? Will you?"

Cringing at the thought of encountering more humans, even short ones, Garry wavered.

"Don't worry," Thaddeus reassured him. "I know of a hidden garden outside of town where it will be safe, and my friends can meet us there to play. They're good blokes, I promise."

Garry gave Thaddeus a gargoyle version of a thumbs-up, trusting the young human.

Thaddeus began to work on a rescue plan for Garry and it didn't take long for him to come up with an idea. Thaddeus's eleventh birthday was in less than a week, and he knew exactly what he would ask for.

"I want Garry for my birthday," he blurted out to his parents during mid-morning tea the Saturday after he spoke with Garry.

"What? Who's Garry?" His mother put down her cup, puzzled.

"Oh... Thaddeus had to think quickly. "Uh...that's what I call the statue you brought home from the antique shoppe."

"You named the gargoyle Garry?"

"Yep! Can I please have him for my birthday?"

"Well Thad, the gargoyle isn't really a toy," his father explained. "You know, the figurine is an antique..."

"Please, Mom? Dad? I've always wanted a gargoyle!" Thaddeus really wanted a new football, but he knew it was the best way to get Garry out of the house.

Surprised, Mr. and Mrs. Stevens beamed at each other. "Well," Mr. Stevens declared, "the statue wasn't perfect when we bought it, so it isn't that valuable. And, you've been a good boy, Thad—so, if the gargoyle is really what you want, you may have it!"

"Thanks!" *Whew! My plan is working!*

The Garden

The garden lay at the edge of Shamlaigh and, like the cathedral where Garry lived, it was a remnant from times gone by. Formidable rock walls swathed in feathery moss surrounded the forgotten place while solid iron gates secured the garden from the outside world.

Upon arriving with his new gargoyle friend, Thaddeus was relieved to find the garden remained abandoned. Garry made the trip through Shamlaigh without incident, this time savoring the sights while riding from the safe bed of Thaddeus's restored Streak-O-Lite red wagon--a gift to Thaddeus from his father, a renowned antique collector, for his eighth birthday.

Garry and Thaddeus pushed against the heavy doors, their rusty hinges creaking as the massive panels labored to swing open. Cautiously, they stepped through the gates into the forsaken garden. A labyrinth of brown grass and tangled, crimson vines dominated the once-treasured haven. A scattering of English daisies rose above the weeds as a reminder of the beauty only their imaginations could now perceive. Flagstone pathways lay buried under ages of accumulated soil as the musty smell of rotting leaves lingered over the unraked grounds.

Scattered debris dishonored the hallowed estate.

Near one corner of the two-acre garden, a single, majestic oak tree stood proudly. Its sturdy trunk and twisting branches supported a dense canopy that extended beyond the garden wall. A limestone fountain marked the center of the expansive courtyard, dry leaves brimmed in its round bowls where water once flowed. Vestiges of the low column that once hosted the fountain's ornamental spout lay decayed and crumbling.

"Oh, my! This is not what I envisioned a garden to be," Garry confessed to Thaddeus.

"This is perfect! No one will come here, and you'll be safe."

Garry still wasn't sure, but at least it was quiet and away from the madness of Shamlaigh.

The following day, Garry met Thaddeus's friends in the garden. Finnlay Payne—whose mother owned the antique shoppe—displayed a thick mop of apple cider hair and vivid shamrock eyes, both features inherited from his father and admired by every girl in school. Freckles sprinkled across his nose belied his porcelain skin, but fit his gregarious nature.

Reginald Essex was the most serious of the three boys. He had a lean, athletic frame, chocolate skin, curly hair, and lush obsidian eyes. A most intelligent lad, Reginald had already mastered all subjects taught two levels above his grade.

Garry the gargoyle had SO much fun frolicking around with the young humans that his desire to return home waned. Being DOWN was looking up! And thus, Garry decided to stay for a while. And when the boys attended school during the day, as well as through the prolonged nights, he posted himself upon the fountain's parched water column, taking the place of the garden's long-gone sentry. From his post, he could see the cathedral steeple rising above Shamlaigh. Garry found unex-pected peace in the garden, and his spirits renewed.

Thaddeus, Reginald, and Finnlay spent many afternoons and weekends playing together with their new mate, Garry the Gargoyle. And even at night, Garry was not alone.

In addition to his human companions, Garry made nighttime friends with the rabbits that ventured out each evening to eat flowers, and bats that darted around in pursuit of a snack under the moonlight. Garry enjoyed the stirring call of the Great Horned Owl's, "Hoot, hoot, hoot!" But, Garry's favorite companion was the shy, yet wise, opossum who meandered from his log home by the garden wall each night. Often, they didn't speak—and, sometimes, they didn't move for hours, enjoying each other's silent company. That made sense, of course, because gargoyles—being statues—and, opossums—famous for playing dead—were experts at staying motionless for long periods of time.

As days and nights passed and spring turned to summer, Garry came to cherish his human friends, and his nocturnal animal friends. Garry was glad he went DOWN.

One evening as Garry counted the shooting stars streaking above him, a dark shadow slunk through the brush below. The movement caught Garry's eye. As he squinted into the moonless night to better evaluate what he saw, he sighted one of his rabbit friends curled up in a ball snoozing soundly not far from the lurking shape.

As Garry's vision came into focus, he recognized the prowler with alarm. The black cat! The very same black cat that had troubled him in the antique shoppe. And that moggy cat was stalking his innocent, sleeping friend!

Oh no you don't, cat! Just as the feline readied to pounce on his unaware victim, Garry sprung into action, leaping from his fountain post to block the black beast's advances on the slumbering rabbit. Startled, the cat halted, yowling in protest of the interrupted hunt. Then, recognizing his foe, the tom raised himself up on his toes, hunching his back with hackles fully extended, attempting to intimidate Garry with his piercing stare. *It's just that silly gargoyle, I can handle him well enough,* thought the cat.

But this time Garry stood his ground and met the cat's gaze. *That cat will not bully me this time!* Garry vowed to himself. And just as the cat began to claw furiously at Garry's stony figure, Garry presented his most ferocious gargoyle face and lunged toward the hissing intruder.

Wide-eyed with terror at seeing the timid gargoyle's countenance suddenly transform into a vision that only nightmares are made of, the cat let out a wild screech and bolted over the garden wall, disappearing into the night.

"*Ah! I am the Lord of the garden! And no one shall threaten this sacred kingdom!*" Garry proclaimed aloud, as the animals cheered, chirped, and squealed, hailing the stone hero for saving their defenseless friend. Rabbit was especially grateful and presented Garry with one of his coveted rhubarb roots in appreciation.

Proudly, Garry stood guard the remainder of the night. He thought of how the other Gargoyles had made fun of him for going to DOWN. *If only they could see me now.*

A New Friend

One afternoon, as the sun's heat radiated with a vengeance, Garry and the boys caught their breath under the refreshing shade of the oak tree after playing a raucous game of tag among the maze of overgrown bushes.

"I'm rather knackered," Garry confessed to the other three as he collapsed under the cool canopy. "Shhh," Thaddeus murmured, hearing branches crackle above them.

The boys squinted into the tree, searching for the source of the movement. "There's a monkey in the tree!" Finnlay proclaimed.

Then came a mysterious giggle.

"That's obviously not a monkey," Reginald stated.

"Who goes there?" Thaddeus yelled toward the oak tree.

"Me," an unknown voice replied.

"Who's me? And what are you doing in that tree?" Reginald demanded answers.

Thaddeus and the others strained to make out the silhouette camouflaged among the verdant leaves.

"This is my tree," said the voice.

"What do you mean, 'your tree'?'" Thaddeus jumped to his feet.

"I come up here to read and not to be bothered."

"Show yourself!" Thaddeus peered up into the tree, issuing his command.

Then, amid rippling leaves and wobbling branches, as effortlessly as a tree squirrel, a sprite of a girl leapt out of the massive oak, standing in defiance before the three boys. With

her ebony hair swinging free, she wore an indigo and lavender plaid skirt and ruby-red tennis shoes with wide, white laces.

A girl! I've never met a girl! How exciting! Garry also stood.

"You can't be here!" Finnlay stamped his foot as the other boys glared at the intruder.

"You can't tell me what to do," the girl countered. "I've been coming to this tree for more than a year!"

"We've never seen you here, and how did you get in without anyone noticing?" Reginald eyed the girl with suspicion.

"You're not here every minute—and besides, I climb the tree from a branch that hangs outside the garden wall."

"Have you been spying on us?" Thaddeus bristled at the thought.

"I have better things to do than spy on a bunch of dumb boys. I told you—I climb the tree to read."

At that moment, the girl noticed Garry fidgeting in the background. "Why, that statue moved!"

With that, Garry squeezed his way through the boys to introduce himself to the girl.

"Hello! My name is Garry—I'm elated to meet you." Garry flashed his infamous gargoyle smile, fangs gleaming in the sun.

Luella did a double take. A stone statue that talks? Wow! "My name is Luella Parsons." Luella's almond-shaped eyes twinkled with charm. "Those are some choppers you've got there…"

"Why, thank you. They're one of my best features."

"Garry, NO! We don't know if we can trust her. She could spoil everything," Thaddeus counseled Garry toward restraint.

The boys stepped in front of Garry, shielding him from Luella.

"You have to leave now—and, you can't tell anyone about what you saw here!" Thaddeus attempted to order Luella, hoping she would go.

"I'm not leaving! This garden doesn't belong to you. Besides, I want to talk to this gargoyle."

"I don't understand," Garry piped up from behind the boys. "Why can't Luella stay? Is something wrong with her?"

"Yes!" Thaddeus clenched his fists with frustration. "She's a girl!"

"Please, Thaddeus," Garry begged. "Can't we keep her? Just for a while?"

"Thank you, Garry," Luella inserted. "Clearly, you're a very nice gargoyle—much nicer than these three boys." She glared at Thaddeus, Finnlay, and Reginald.

"What do you read up there in that tree, Luella?" Garry pushed his way through the boys.

"Fantasy and history. I know it's an odd combination, but it's what I'm keen on," Luella admitted not-so-shyly.

"Hmmm... we should get along tickety-boo then." Garry danced a little jig.

Thaddeus finally gave in. "Okay! Fine. Luella can stay..."

"Yippee!" Garry grinned, his fangs front and center. Thaddeus, Reginald, and Finnlay groaned while Luella twirled a pirouette.

And, just like that, Garry's clan of human friends grew and, as it turned out, Luella and the boys got along swell. Luella not only demonstrated herself to be an exceptional tree-climber, she also proved her skill at knucklebones, one of the boys' favorite pastimes.

The following Saturday, the boys and Luella decided to teach Garry how to play the game of kick the can. "It's simple, Garry—you just run, then kick the can with your foot as hard as possible," Thaddeus explained as he placed the beat up tin in the center of a patch of dirt. "The idea is to keep the can away from the other team until you or a teammate can kick it across the goal line." He paused, looking at Garry. "Why don't you try it?"

This game sounds jolly—and, it certainly can't be too difficult, Garry thought, backing away from the can to ensure he could gain sufficient momentum to send the target flying. He so desired to impress his friends.

Garry sped toward the can and, as he closed in on the rusty object, he swung his right leg behind him, and then thrust his foot forward with excellent aim. However, as Garry's toes flung the tin high into the air, his whole body followed in pursuit!

Luella and the boys stared as their friend flipped in a heels-over-head somersault before landing with a THUNK on his back. A second later, the can descended from the sky, bouncing off Garry's forehead before careening to a stop in the dirt a few inches away. With mouths agape, the kids watched as Garry lay confounded on the ground. "Perhaps I am better suited for spewing rainwater than I am for kicking cans," Garry commented casually, hopping to his feet.

The boys and Luella erupted in laughter and Garry joined in the chorus, his pointed ears raised, wiggling with glee.

The Gargoyle Chronicles

Luella, Thaddeus, Reginald, and Finnlay jam-packed their days with games of one kind or another—but, their favorite activity centered around Garry as they huddled in the courtyard to listen to stories of long ago. Garry sat with his mates, telling tales of all he saw in his early years atop the church. Garry witnessed a great deal over the centuries, recalling lively street markets, spirited trading, grand battles, and lavish celebrations.

"Why are gargoyles on the church, Garry?" Reginald's desire to learn more grew with each new episode.

"We were sculpted as decorative waterspouts to funnel rainwater away from the age-old buildings through our mouths," he answered as his friends giggled, envisioning spitting gargoyles.

"We should have a spitting contest!" Finnlay announced.

"Nah, Garry would win every time..." Reginald made clear as Luella pursed her lips in disgust of the idea.

"Do you have other stories about the knights and princesses, Garry?" Thaddeus begged his friend to tell them more about days gone by.

Luella and the other boys nodded in encouragement, and Garry knew exactly the story to delight his audience.

"Long ago," he began, "in the village streets, the annual jousting festival took place. Regal knights and brave lords battled for the hands of the kingdom's finest ladies. Only the most courageous men in all the realm competed." He paused, recalling the wondrous scene. "Villagers and farmers," he continued, "whether rich or poor, assembled from all over the countryside to cheer for their favorite lord or knight."

Garry's friends listened intently, hanging on every word.

"Adorned in heavy, silver armor," Garry recalled, "knights and lords rode upon splendid horses that pranced and snorted in anticipation of the royal games. Crowds waved flags of scarlet and purple—the colors of the crown—and then, as trumpets blared, the steeds broke into a gallop. The armored contestants charged toward each other, their jousting poles crash-

ing into their opponents, knocking one or the other from his mount until one victorious rider remained. The crowd stood and roared in applause!"

"What happened next?" Luella asked, her eyes wide.

"Well, as tradition dictated, the winner of each match presented himself on one knee to the maiden of his choice. Silence gripped the village. Would the fair maiden accept the dashing knight with a single nod? Or send him away with a flick of her wrist? The decision was hers..." No one said anything, waiting for Garry to continue.

"The festival carried on for two full days. Animated mimes performed, and lively music echoed in the streets as folks danced and sang throughout the township. It was a splendid sight to behold!"

All of the kids clapped and hollered, and then Luella's eyes grew misty. "Did you really see all of that yourself, Garry? Way up there?"

Garry nodded. "Yes—gargoyles have superb vision. That's why we can see spirits, good or bad, sometimes tarrying near the church or building we're charged with protecting. The same thing is true for grotesques."

Finnlay half-repeated the word. "Grow–what?"

"Gro-tes-ques. They also live on the cathedral walls—however, they don't have the ability to funnel water. Today, their sole purpose is to ward off evil spirits. In medieval times, though, the kingdom's rulers used grotesques with their gnarled faces to intimidate their subjects."

"Wow!" Finnlay and Reginald exclaimed in unison.

"What about your wings?" Finnlay asked, fascinated. "Can you fly?"

Garry's mood shifted. "A winged gargoyle is only supposed to fly during battles with those maleficent spirits menacing the cathedral. We are not allowed to let humans see us fly, and we are not to speak of such encounters."

The kids sat quietly for a moment, absorbing Garry's words.

Reginald, meditated upon the logic of Garry's claims, and probed further. "Your wings seem too small for your heavy stone body to fly…"

"Anything is possible, Reginald, if you believe." Garry sought to put the subject to rest. But sensing the kids relentless intrigue with his wings, Garry surrendered, deciding to share the tale of all gargoyle tales—the dramatic, little-known origin story of gargoyles. "I am one of a select few gargoyles of my time who has wings. Legend has it, gargoyles carved with the ability to fly are created in likeness of the first gargoyle—who just so happened to be a fire-breathing, water-breathing dragon!"

"A dragon! How spectacular!" Finnlay glanced at his friends, then settled in for more. Thad also made himself more comfortable. "Tell us about the dragon, Garry."

The kids gathered closer as Garry shared the mythical tale of La Gargouille. "La Gargouille, a most unpleasant dragon, had bat-like wings, sharp curved horns, and enormous glowing amber eyes. For hundreds of years, he roamed the French countryside terrorizing the people of the port village of Rouen." Garry paused, mostly for drama. "The reptilian monster was said to have swallowed whole ships, burned the lands, and flooded the town with water from the Seine River!"

The boys sat, unblinking, mesmerized by Garry's story while Luella, unnerved by the chronicle, twisted the laces of her trademark red sneakers in her fingertips.

"Eventually," Garry continued, "the wretched dragon was captured by Romanus, the town's priest, who led the creature to the village square."

"What happened then?" Thaddeus couldn't take his eyes off of his friend.

Garry looked at each of them, his voice low, almost a whisper. "He was set on fire! The dragon's head, however, survived the blaze, so the villagers placed his slain crown high on the wall of the church as a warning to other invading dragons." There was barely a sound as the kids held their breath.

"Then," Garry continued, "something quite remarkable happened. When the rain fell, water flowed down from the roof into the dragon's head, out through his mouth, and away from the building. And, according to folklore, the first gargoyle was born—and we have been protecting church masonry from rainwater ever since!"

"You may have wings and horns, Garry, but you're nothing like that dreadful dragon," Luella decreed, compelled to clarify the difference in character between the two.

"Well, I think it's utterly fantastic! Imagine... Garry, part dragon," Finnlay piped in, a far-away look in his eyes.

"And, I, for one, do fancy a good fable..." Luella curtsied to Garry in appreciation.

Thaddeus could barely believe it. "Who named you, Garry?"

"I believe I was named by the mason who carved me. My formal name is Garrett, Gargoyle Garrett." He bowed with pride.

"Do the other gargoyles have names," Thaddeus asked.

"Why, yes, they do. Clovis, Ezekiel, Adrian, and Falco, to name a few—and, of course, Luke and Leopold. Luke and Leopold are swarmy—always causing trouble, and playing tricks on the other gargoyles."

"Tell us more, Garry! Tell us about Luke and Leopold," Reginald pleaded, the others backing him up.

Garry agreed. However, the setting sun dictated it was time for the kids to return home. Thus, the story of Luke and Leopold would have to wait for a new day when the gang gathered again in the garden of friends.

Luke and Leopold

"Luke and Leopold are notorious among gargoyles to this day," Garry began the next morning, relishing his new role as storyteller. "One incident took place four hundred years ago in early spring." He paused, looking at each of his entranced subjects. "After it rained buckets and buckets upon the land, Luke and Leopold clambered down to collect tadpoles from the water puddles that accumulated near the base of the church.

"That same night, they paid Clovis—who lives two levels down from Luke and Leopold—a visit. While Luke distracted Clovis with witty conversation, Leopold dropped the tadpoles into the trough in Clovis's back where the rainwater collects. Well, there was enough water for the tadpoles to live, but not enough for them to swim out of Clovis's spout. So, over the next several weeks, the tadpoles grew, turning into full-grown frogs. But Clovis had no idea that anything was skew-whiff.

"The next time it rained, everyone in the whole church heard Clovis screech in terror as dozens of green frogs flew out of his mouth. Clovis was convinced he was possessed by demons as the frogs continued to gush through his rain spout!"

Luella clutched her belly, howling in hysterics along with the boys. "Not a single gargoyle or grotesque was silent that night," Garry contin-

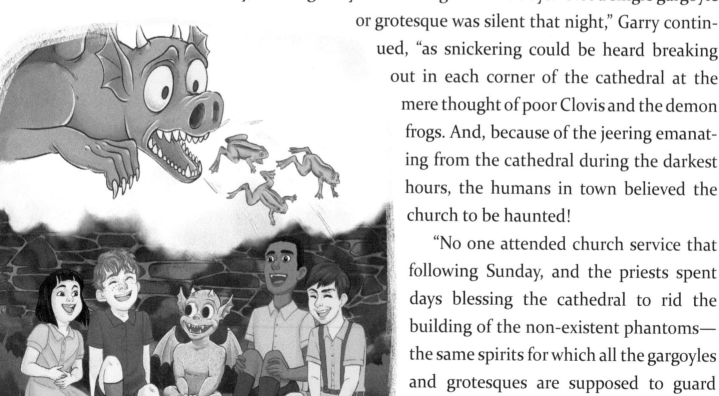

ued, "as snickering could be heard breaking out in each corner of the cathedral at the mere thought of poor Clovis and the demon frogs. And, because of the jeering emanating from the cathedral during the darkest hours, the humans in town believed the church to be haunted!

"No one attended church service that following Sunday, and the priests spent days blessing the cathedral to rid the building of the non-existent phantoms—the same spirits for which all the gargoyles and grotesques are supposed to guard against." Garry shook his head. "It was a definitely a dog's dinner—and, no . . . Luke and Leopold are not well-behaved gargoyles."

Luella grimaced. "Did Luke and Leopold ever bother you, Garry?"

"I was too high up for Luke and Leopold to bother—but, their mischief throughout the centuries continues to this day."

As the four friends pleaded with Garry to share more about his life, he was overcome with joy. And, it was then Garry realized he was not simply an old relic of a forgotten past—he was a testament to a meaningful history.

Garry no longer mourned what was gone, but was happy for today.

The garden came alive during that summer as Luella and the boys transformed the neglected site into an enchanted land of laughter and ingenuity. Overgrown shrubs became fortresses for the princely young lords. Fallen tree branches served as mighty horses for the brave knights. Tangled vines provided fine locks of long golden hair, while dried berries mimicked jewels for princess Luella's crown.

The courtyard became the place of royal games with Garry poised on the dry fountain portraying the evil La Gargouille that threatened the kingdom. Even the animals of the garden joined in the performances. Through Garry, the rabbits, squirrels, and birds began to trust the humans, and only the bashful opossum remained reluctant as he watched from the safe sidelines of his hollow log. The animals romped, frisked, and leaped with delight as the children lost themselves in fanciful play.

Through his five hundred and two years, Garry experienced many summers.

But, that one would forever be his favorite.

Going Home

Weeks came and went, and daylight shortened as shadows shifted from summer to autumn. Thaddeus, Finnlay, Reginald, and Luella went back to school and, even though Garry had his animal friends to keep him company, he felt a disquiet building inside of him.

One gloomy day, as Garry idled upon the broken-down column of the waterless fountain, pelting raindrops began to fall from the sky—SPLAT! The rain bounced off of Garry's head. *Oh, no! The church steeple!* As the rain fell harder, Garry fretted about not performing his duty as a gargoyle, straining to see the cathedral through thickening clouds. Then for the first time since arriving at the garden, Garry felt...

Homesick.

He ached for his steeple home, and he knew the time had come to return to UP. But, he also knew it would be difficult to leave his animal friends as well as his human friends behind. Most of all... Thaddeus.

"It's time for me to go home..." Garry's voice hitched with emotion as he informed his companions of his decision later that day. "I miss my life as a gargoyle, and I miss my gaff—the rains have returned, and it's my responsibility to safeguard the church walls. That's why I exist..."

Thaddeus gazed at Garry with woeful eyes as magical memories of the summer past flooded his thoughts. Luella wept in sorrow as she wrapped her slender arms around Garry.

None of the kids wanted him to go, and they would miss their waggish friend. But, they understood.

Reginald and Finnlay bid Garry a cheery good-bye, each giving him a quick pat on the head as they wished him luck on his return home. Luella, especially heartbroken to see her gargoyle friend go, leaned over and gently kissed Garry on his cheek—if stone statues could blush, Garry would have turned quite pink.

Before the sun rose the following morning, Garry once again climbed into Thaddeus's little red wagon, folding his wings in tightly as Thaddeus covered him with a mauve and cobalt quilt to avoid drawing attention from nosey onlookers already on their way to work. The operating headlights of the Radio Flyer, made navigating the sidewalk in the predawn hours easier. It's rusty wheels squeaked with each turn as Thaddeus hauled Garry to his destination.

Once at the base of the historic cathedral in Shamlaigh, Garry the gargoyle vaulted to the sidewalk, contemplating UP.

Home.

A single tear swelled in the corner of Garry's eye. "I will always watch over you, Thaddeus—and, I'll never forget you, and our garden of friends."

"I will miss you more than all of the stars in the galaxy, Gargoyle Garrett—and, every time I look at that big ol' cathedral, I'll think of you way up there." Thaddeus paused, sniffling. "Say hi to the other gargoyles for me..."

Garry squeezed his stony arms around Thaddeus's legs, then clambered up the steps to embark upon his journey home.

Thaddeus kept Garry in his sight as he scaled the soaring cathedral. When he could no longer see his extraordinary friend, he saluted Garry one last time.

Though the time had come to say goodbye, the upside-down adventure over, Garry and Thaddeus knew they would always be friends. Garry would forever be UP, looking DOWN, and, Thaddeus, would forever be DOWN, looking UP.

Pip-pip for now!

Glossary

Cantie: Pleasant, lively, cheerful. Origin: Cantie is an early 1700s Scottish Gaelic term. It is reasoned that this term derived from the Low German word kant or kanty, which has a similar meaning.

Collywobbles: Extreme queasiness or stomach pain brought on by stress, nervousness, or anxiety. Origin: The earliest known use of this term was in 1823, and is believed to have been derived from colic, a severe fluctuating pain in the stomach due to gas or obstruction, and wobble, meaning to be unstable or wobble.

Daft: Unwise, mad, foolish, stupid. Origin: This term comes from the Middle English daffte, daft, defte, meaning well-mannered, gentle, dull, foolish. This term goes back to Old English, gedæfte, meaning gentle, mild, meek. One speculation regarding the leap from well-meaning and gentle to foolish is a result of early cultural belief that gentle and meek people were mad, and so are those who are too trustful.

Doddle: An easy task. Origin: This informal British term is from the early 1900s. It is believed to have been derived from toddle or toddler, referring to the saying, It's as easy as child's play.

Dog's dinner: A mess or fiasco. Origin: This is an English term formed in the late 1800s. It is surmised that this term is in reference to a dog's meal, which, in those days, was a messy concoction of different byproducts of human food.

Gaff: An informal British word for home. Origin: Gaff is the Middle English term for where one lives. The word is derived from the use of gaff in the eighteenth century, meaning a cheap music hall or theatre.

Gobsmacked: Amazed or awed by something, astounded, bewildered, shocked. Origin: This term has its roots in coal mining lingo from as early as the mid-1700s. A 'gob' is a term used in reference to an old coal mining pit or dangerous space left behind by mining, and the term was adopted in New South Wales in the early 1800s by coal miners of that era. Thus, it is believed that the term 'gob' evolved to mean surprise or shock at unintentionally falling into an abandoned coal mine pit or mouth. By the early 1900s, 'gobsmacked' was a popularly coined slang term used by the Northern English and Scottish. 'Gob' refers to mouth, and, combined with 'smack,' the term 'gobsmacked' refers to the action of clapping one's hand over one's mouth in astonishment.

Good old chinwag: A good chat, catching up, or gossip with someone. Origin: Good old chinwag is an informal British term relating to a wagging or moving chin when speaking.

Knackered: Tired, beat, or exhausted, often uttered after a strenuous activity or a long day. Origin: This term is believed to first have been used in the sixteenth century. Knack means trinket, originally denoting a harness-maker.

Knucklebones: An early form of the game of Jacks, in which any small object or combination of objects may be used for jacks: stones, bones, pieces of wood, or metal jacks. Origin: The term knucklebones is of ancient origin. In the early version of knucklebones, the jacks were small bones from the hocks of sheep called the astragalus.

Moggy: Mongrel cat. Origin: This term has Cockney origins referring to an alley cat without pedigree. It became more popular in the early 1900s.

Pip-pip: Archaic, out-of-use phrase used to say good-bye. Origin: Pip-pip is an early 1900s British term. It is speculated to have been derived from the sound of bicycle horns or car horns often tooted twice in a gesture meaning good-bye as someone rode or drove away.

Skew-whiff: Askew or awry. Origin: This mid-eighteenth-century term came together from 'skew', meaning askew, and 'whiff', meaning puff of air.

Shambles: A disorganized mess or chaotic environment. Origin: Shambles is a fifteenth century reference to a meat or fish market. This term is a derivation from schamil, Old English for table or stall for vending. By the 1590s the term referred to a place of butchery, thus the reference to confusion and mess.

Swarmy: Scheming or untrustworthy. Origin: The time period of the origin of the term 'swarmy' is unknown. It has its roots in British maritime history, particularly known for use in pirate lingo. Related to swarmy is the term smarmy, an early 1900s derivation.

Tickety-boo: Satisfactory, well, and in good order. Origin: This term is possibly related to the Hindi word 'hīk hai,' meaning 'it's all right.' Tickety-boo is chiefly a British slang word used since the nineteenth century.

Waggish: Humorous in a playful way, comical. Origin: This term is believed to have first been used in 1589. Waggish is derived from 'wag,' meaning a person who is hilarious, and keeps one entertained by witty stories.

Acknowledgments

After my mom's passing, I discovered the handwritten, partial manuscript of *Garry The Gargoyle* buried among her keepsakes in an old, worn cardboard box. Upon first reading her scratched notes, I knew Garry was special. I also knew the vision of Garry needed to come to life.

Nearly twenty years later, *The Adventures Of Garry The Gargoyle* has arrived in full splendor for children and parents around the world to enjoy! And now this revised version brings new and enhanced magic to Garry's story.

Many have commented, "What a wonderful gift finishing Garry is for your mother..." But, through the process of writing this magical story, I realized I'm the true recipient of the gift.

Thank you to my mom, Mary Christenson Wyman.

It is only with the tremendous support of some extraordinary people that this book is complete. Thank you to my husband, George Vardaman, who believed in me, this story, and the need to honor my mom's vision.

I thank my siblings, George and Christen, who have been my life-long support, and whom I love with all of my heart. Thank you to my brother John, who inspires me though his music and exceptional spirit. And, thank you to my 'new' sister, Julie, for finding us and bringing such joy into our lives!

I am tremendously grateful to Paulette Kinnes, editor of the first edition who taught me so much and invested so deeply in Garry.

For this revised edition, I thank Susan Schader, who renewed my confidence in my own voice and writing style, and helped to bring Book i to its full potential.

A huge thank you to Paisley Hansen, the fabulous illustrator who brought form, color, and character to Garry and all of his friends. It was a true honor to work with such talent and genius.

I wish to express huge thanks to Robin Surface of Fideli Publishing Inc., for her kind advice, professionalism, patience, and for going above and beyond with the layout revisions, printing, and publishing of this book.

Thank you to my dear friend, Christina Souto, for her endless wisdom, support, and expertise in crafting the website, as well as other promotional materials for this book.

And, finally, I thank Will Owens—the remarkable young boy whose ideas and creativity helped bring more fun and life to this story.

Professional Acknowledgments

PUBLISHER and BOOK DESIGNER

Fedeli Publishing, Inc
Robin Surface
www.fedelipublishing.com

EDITORS

Platinum Editing Group, LLC
Paulette K. Kinnes, Editor
paulette@platinumeditinggroup.com

Story Services for Writers
Susan Schader, Editor, Story Analyst, Consultant
www.StoryServicesForWriters.com

ILLUSTRATOR
Paisley Hansen

CONTRIBUTING ILLUSTRATOR
Michael Dee
www.MichaelDee.com

PRODUCED BY
Shamlaigh Media

About the Author...

Born and raised in Laguna Beach, California, Karin's love of the ocean inspired her to study Marine Science in California and Mexico. Karin spent most of her career in environmental education and non- profit leadership with a focus on marine conservation and maritime history. While in California she obtained her 100- ton Coast Guard Certified Captain's license and sailed tallships off California's Channel Islands for nearly 24 years. She also competed in open ocean distance swims, as well as local sprint triathlons.

In 2011, her passion turned to the wild wolf and, during the last nine years, Karin has become a leader in wolf conservation, focusing on mitigating wolf-livestock conflicts. Because of her important work, Karin was highlighted in the July 9, 2019 issue of The New Yorker Magazine, "The Persuasive Power of the Wolf Lady."

An avid writer since childhood, Karin writes professionally and personally, penning two national, award-winning education programs. Because of her background in education, she aspired to write a children's book not only designed to spark imagination, but to provide an educational element, as well. Her goal was to weave historical detail, fun vocabulary, and a few life lessons into a whimsical story filled with adventure that will put a smile on any child's or parent's face.

Garry's Upside-Down Adventure is the cornerstone book in The Adventures Of Garry The Gargoyle Series. Book 2, *Garry's Heroic Adventure*, is expected to launch in 2021!

Karin now resides in Indian Hills, Colorado enjoying hiking the Rocky Mountains and slalom waterskiing near her home.

You can contact her: info@garrythegargoyle.com.

Please visit Garry's website at:

www.GarryTheGargoyle.com

Coming in 2021...

Garry's Heroic Adventure

The Adventures Of Garry The Gargoyle Series, Book 2

For more fun with Garry, please visit
www.GarryTheGargoyle.com

CPSIA information can be obtained
at www.ICGtesting.com
Printed in the USA
LVHW071523280322
714606LV00013B/1021